Dear Friends,

As a young boy, I was not a wonderful student. I loved my art classes and I also loved learning about animals, insects, and the wonders of nature — but I have to confess that I hated some other subjects, like arithmetic, though I knew they were important. Now, in the picture books I make for children — and for the child in me — I often combine the things I loved with the things I hated.

It bored me when my teacher demanded that I learn that 2 + 2 = 4. I wish my teacher had said, "One fine morning two green fish and two brown frogs met in a lily pond. One of the green fish said to one of the brown frogs..." etc. I can assure you that I would have remembered forever and with delight the sum of 2 + 2.

The three stories in this book are based on this simple observation. All can be enjoyed just for the entertaining plots and colorful pictures alone. But in each I have also incorporated some important learning. All three tell something about time — the time of day, the months of the year, and the changing seasons. Each celebrates nature, but contains other lessons, too.

*Rooster's Off to See the World* is about addition and subtraction, about various kinds of animals; it is also about curiosity, the urge to explore, and the difference between fantasy and reality.

*A House for Hermit Crab* is about the twelve months, about symbiosis, about creativity, and about adapting to growth and change.

*The Tiny Seed* is about subtraction; it is also about the life cycle of plants. It shows that nature may sometimes seem cruel, but in the end gives us life, growth, beauty, and joy.

I feel fortunate that my love for my long-ago art classes has enabled me today to make these pictures and tell these stories.

Enjoy!

*Eric Carle*

# STORIES FOR ALL SEASONS
## BY ERIC CARLE

*Rooster's Off to See the World*
*A House for Hermit Crab*
*The Tiny Seed*

*Simon & Schuster Books for Young Readers*

*For Benjamin*

SIMON & SCHUSTER BOOKS FOR YOUNG READERS
An imprint of Simon & Schuster Children's Publishing Division
1230 Avenue of the Americas, New York, New York 10020

Book design and title lettering by Eric Carle
The text for this book is set in Veljovic.
The illustrations are rendered in painted tissue paper collage.

Printed in the United States of America

First Edition

10 9 8 7 6 5 4 3 2 1

Library of Congress Card Catalog Number: 98-60299

# ROOSTER'S OFF TO SEE THE WORLD

One fine morning, a rooster decided that he wanted to travel.
So, right then and there, he set out to see the world.
He hadn't walked very far when he began to feel lonely.

Just then, he met two cats. The rooster said to them,
"Come along with me to see the world."
The cats liked the idea of a trip very much.
"We would love to," they purred and set off down
the road with the rooster.

As they wandered on,
the rooster and the cats met three frogs.
"How would you like to come with us to see the world?"
asked the rooster, eager for more company.
"Why not?" answered the frogs.
"We are not busy now." So the frogs jumped
along behind the rooster and the cats.

After a while, the rooster, the cats, and the frogs
saw four turtles crawling slowly down the road.
"Hey," said the rooster,
"how would you like to see the world?"
"It might be fun," snapped one of the turtles
and they joined the others.

As the rooster, the cats, the frogs, and the turtles walked
along, they came to five fish swimming in the brook.
"Where are you going?" asked the fish.
"We're off to see the world," answered the rooster.
"May we come along?" pleaded the fish.
"Delighted to have you," the rooster replied.
And so the fish came along
to see the world.

The sun went down. It began to get dark. The moon came
up over the horizon. "Where's our dinner?" asked the cats.
"Where are we supposed to sleep?" asked the frogs.
"We're cold," complained the turtles.

Just then, some fireflies flew overhead. "We're afraid," cried the fish.
Now, the rooster really had not made any plans for the trip around
the world. He had not remembered to think about food and shelter,
so he didn't know how to answer his friends.

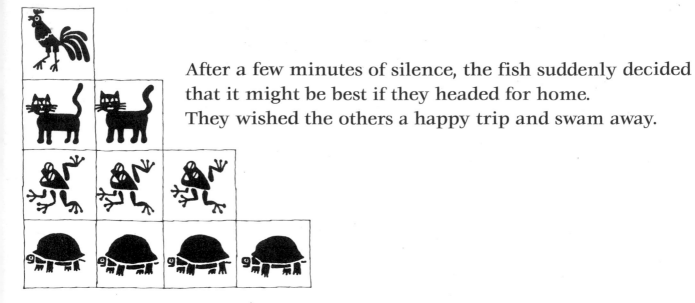

After a few minutes of silence, the fish suddenly decided
that it might be best if they headed for home.
They wished the others a happy trip and swam away.

Then, the turtles began to think about their warm house. They turned and crawled back down the road without so much as a good-bye.

The frogs weren't too happy with the trip anymore, either. First one and then the other and finally the last one jumped away. They were polite enough, though, to wish the rooster a good evening as they disappeared into the night.

The cats then remembered an unfinished meal
they had left behind. They kindly wished the rooster
a happy journey and they, too, headed for home.

Now the rooster was all alone — and he hadn't seen
anything of the world. He thought for a minute and then
said to the moon, "To tell you the truth, I am not only
hungry and cold, but I'm homesick as well."
The moon did not answer. It, too, disappeared.

The rooster knew what he had to do.
He turned around and went back home again.
He enjoyed a good meal of grain and then sat on his very own perch.

After a while he went to sleep and had a wonderful
happy dream–all about a trip around the world!

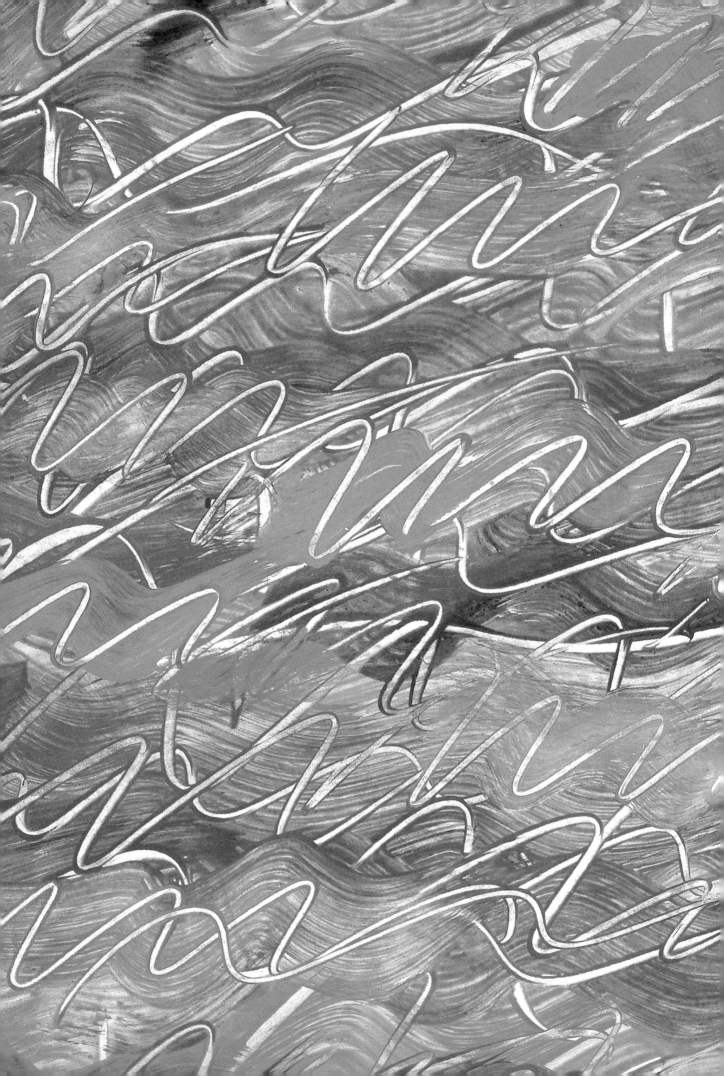

*Hermit Crabs live
on the ocean floor.
Their skin is hard,
except for the abdomen,
which is soft.*

*To protect this "soft spot"
the hermit crab
borrows a shell and
makes this its "house."*

*Then only its face,
feet and claws stick out
from the shell.
That way, it can see,
walk and catch its food.*

*When a hermit crab
is threatened, it withdraws
into its shell until the
danger has passed.*

# A HOUSE FOR HERMIT CRAB

"Time to move," said Hermit Crab one day in January.
"I've grown too big for this little shell."

He had felt safe and snug in his shell. But now it was too snug.
Hermit Crab stepped out of the shell and onto the floor of the ocean.
But it was frightening out in the open sea without a shell to hide in.

"What if a big fish comes along and attacks me?" he thought.
"I must find a new house soon."

Early in February, Hermit Crab found just the house he was looking for. It was a big shell, and strong. He moved right in, wiggling and waggling about inside it to see how it felt. It felt just right.

"But it looks so–well, so *plain*," thought Hermit Crab.

In March, Hermit Crab met some sea anemones.
They swayed gently back and forth in the water.

"How beautiful you are!" said Hermit Crab.
"Would one of you be willing to come and live on my house?
  It is so plain, it needs you."

"I'll come," whispered a small sea anemone.

  Gently, Hermit Crab picked it up with his claw
  and put it on his shell.

In April, Hermit Crab passed a flock of starfish moving slowly along the sea floor.

"How handsome you are!" said Hermit Crab.
"Would one of you be willing to decorate my house?"

"I would," signalled a little sea star.

Carefully, Hermit Crab picked it up with his claw and put it on his house.

In May, Hermit Crab discovered some coral.
They were hard, and didn't move.

"How pretty you are!" said Hermit Crab.
"Would one of you be willing to help
make my house more beautiful?"

"I would," creaked a crusty coral.

Gingerly, Hermit Crab picked it up with his claw and placed it on his shell.

In June, Hermit Crab came to a group of snails crawling over a rock on the ocean floor. They grazed as they went, picking up algae and bits of debris, and leaving a neat path behind them.

"How tidy and hard-working you are!" said Hermit Crab. "Would one of you be willing to come and help clean my house?"

"I would," offered one of the snails.

Happily, Hermit Crab picked it up with his claw and placed it on his shell.

In July, Hermit Crab came upon several sea urchins.
They had sharp, prickly needles.

"How fierce you look!" said Hermit Crab.
"Would one of you be willing to protect my house?"

"I would," answered a spiky sea urchin.

Gratefully, Hermit Crab picked it up with his claw
and placed it near his shell.

In August, Hermit Crab and his friends wandered into
a forest of seaweed. "It's so dark here," thought Hermit Crab.
"How dim it is," murmured the sea anemone.
"How gloomy it is," whispered the starfish.
"How murky it is," complained the coral.
"I can't see!" said the snail.
"It's like nighttime!" cried the sea urchin.

In September, Hermit Crab spotted a school of lanternfish darting through the dark water.

"How bright you are!" said Hermit Crab.
"Would one of you be willing to light up our house?"

"I would," replied one lanternfish. And it swam over near the shell.

In October, Hermit Crab approached a pile of smooth pebbles.

"How sturdy you are!" said Hermit Crab.
"Would you mind if I rearranged you?"

"Not at all," answered the pebbles.

Hermit Crab picked them up one by one with his claw
and built a wall around his shell.

"Now my house is perfect!" cheered Hermit Crab.

But in November, Hermit Crab felt that his shell seemed a bit
too small. Little by little, over the year, Hermit Crab had grown.
Soon he would have to find another, bigger home.
But he had come to love his friends, the sea anemone,
the starfish, the coral, the sea urchin, the snail, the lanternfish,
and even the smooth pebbles.

"They have been so good to me," thought Hermit Crab.
"They are like a family. How can I ever leave them?"

In December, a smaller hermit crab passed by.

"I have outgrown my shell," she said.
"Would you know of a place for me?"

"I have outgrown *my* house, too," answered Hermit Crab.
"I must move on. You are welcome to live here—
but you must promise to be good to my friends."

"I promise," said the little crab.

The following January,
Hermit Crab stepped out and the little crab moved in.

"Couldn't stay in that little shell forever,"
said Hermit Crab as he waved goodbye.

The ocean floor looked wider
than he had remembered,
but Hermit Crab wasn't afraid.
Soon he spied the perfect house–
a big, empty shell. It looked, well,
a little plain, but...

"Sponges!" he thought.
"Barnacles! Clown fish! Sand dollars! Electric eels!
Oh, there are so many possibilities!
I can't wait to get started!"

***Sea Anemones*** may look like flowers, but they are soft animals (polyps) without bony skeletons. They come in many shapes and colors. With their many arms (tentacles) they catch their prey. Some specialize in attaching themselves to the shell of the hermit crab. Then they protect and camouflage the hermit crab, and, in turn, may share the hermit crab's meals. This arrangement is called symbiosis, meaning that both animals benefit from each other.

***Starfish.*** There are many kinds of starfish. Most have five arms growing from a central disk. The mouth of a starfish is on the underside of this disk, and it has a single, simple eye on the end of each arm. With its powerful arms it can open an oyster, or hold onto a rock during a storm when the waves lash about.

***Corals*** are somewhat similar to tiny sea anemones that build hard skeletons around themselves. Then hundreds and hundreds of them stick together, forming whole colonies. Some look like branches; others are round or disk-like. Millions upon millions fuse themselves together to build miles-long coral reefs. Some, however, live by themselves.

***Snails.*** There are approximately 80,000 species of snails and slugs. Some live on land, others live in the sea or in lakes. Some carry a shell–their "houses"–on their backs; others have none. The shells come in many colors and shapes.

***Sea Urchins.*** Some are fat and round, others are thin and spindly. Many have long spines (sometimes poisonous) with which they move around and dig into the mud or rocks or other places. Their mouths, with five pointed teeth, are on the underside.

***Lanternfish,*** like fireflies, have luminous, or light-producing, spots on their bodies that light up their dark surroundings. Some lanternfish have a lantern-like organ that dangles in front of their mouths, attracting other fish which become their prey.

*For Ann Beneduce*

# THE TINY SEED

It is Autumn.
A strong wind is blowing. It blows flower seeds high in the air and carries them far across the land. One of the seeds is tiny, smaller than any of the others. Will it be able to keep up with the others? And where are they all going?

One of the seeds flies higher than the others. Up, up it goes!
It flies too high and the sun's hot rays burn it up.
But the tiny seed sails on with the others.

Another seed lands on a tall and icy mountain.
The ice never melts, and the seed cannot grow.
The rest of the seeds fly on. But the tiny seed does not
go as fast as the others.

Now they fly over the ocean. One seed falls into the water and drowns. The others sail on with the wind. But the tiny seed does not go as high as the others.

One seed drifts down onto the desert. It is hot and dry,
and the seed cannot grow. Now the tiny seed is flying very low,
but the wind pushes it on with the others.

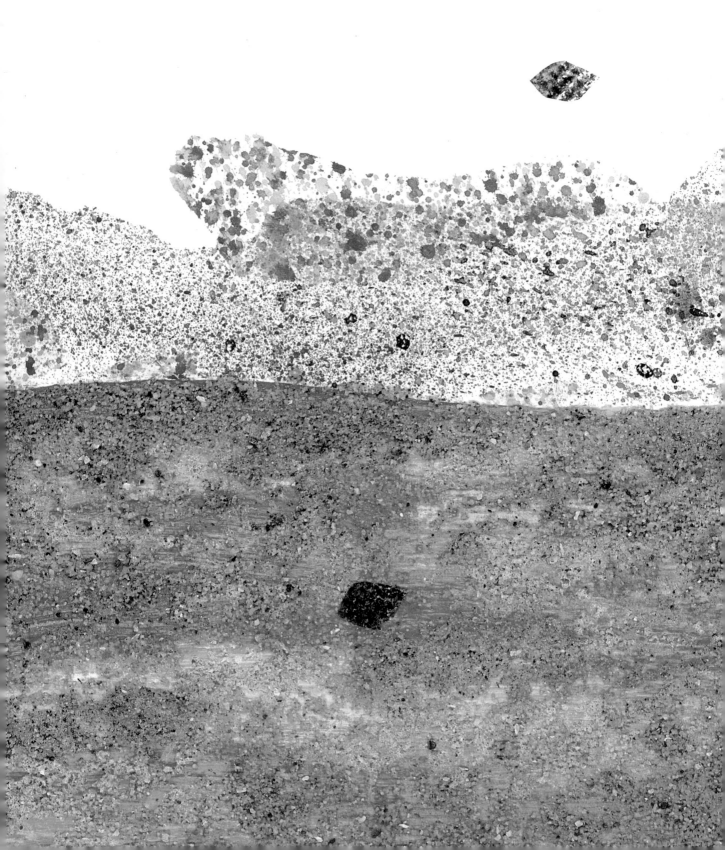

Finally the wind stops and the seeds fall gently down on the ground. A bird comes by and eats one seed. The tiny seed is not eaten. It is so small that the bird does not see it.

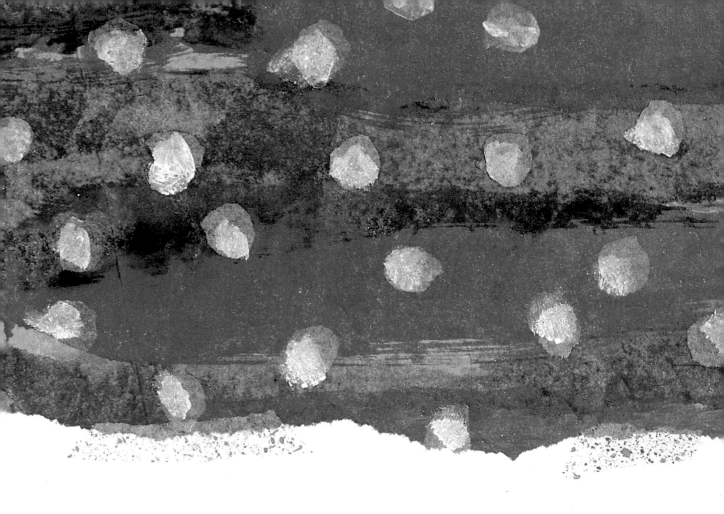

Now it is Winter.
After their long trip the seeds settle down. They look just as if
they are going to sleep in the earth. Snow falls and covers them
like a soft white blanket. A hungry mouse that also lives in
the ground eats a seed for his lunch.
But the tiny seed lies very still and the mouse does not see it.

Now it is Spring.

After a few months the snow has melted. It is really spring!

Birds fly by. The sun shines. Rain falls. The seeds grow so round and full they start to burst open a little.

Now they are not seeds any more. They are plants.

First they send roots down into the earth. Then their little stems and leaves begin to grow up toward the sun and air.

There is another plant that grows much faster than the new little plants. It is a big fat weed. And it takes all the sunlight and the rain away from one of the small new plants. And that little plant dies.

The tiny seed hasn't begun to grow yet. It will be too late! Hurry! But finally it too starts to grow into a plant.

The warm weather also brings the children out to play.
They too have been waiting for the sun and spring time.
One child doesn't see the plants as he runs along and —
Oh! He breaks one! Now it cannot grow any more.

The tiny plant that grew from the tiny seed is growing fast, but its neighbor grows even faster. Before the tiny plant has three leaves the other plant has seven! And look! A bud! And now even a flower!

But what is happening? First there are footsteps.
Then a shadow looms over them.
Then a hand reaches down and breaks off the flower.

A boy has picked the flower to give to a friend.

It is Summer.
Now the tiny plant from the tiny seed is all alone.
It grows on and on. It doesn't stop. The sun shines on it
and the rain waters it. It has many leaves.
It grows taller and taller. It is taller than the people.
It is taller than the trees. It is taller than the houses.
And now a flower grows on it. People come from far and near
to look at this flower. It is the tallest flower they have ever seen.
It is a giant flower.

All summer long the birds and bees and butterflies come visiting.
They have never seen such a big and beautiful flower.

Now it is Autumn again.
The days grow shorter. The nights grow cooler.
And the wind carries yellow and red leaves past the flower.
Some petals drop from the giant flower and they sail along with
the bright leaves over the land and down to the ground.

The wind blows harder. The flower has lost almost all of its petals.
It sways and bends away from the wind. But the wind grows
stronger and shakes the flower. Once more the wind shakes
the flower, and this time the flower's seed pod opens.
Out come many tiny seeds that quickly sail far away on the wind.

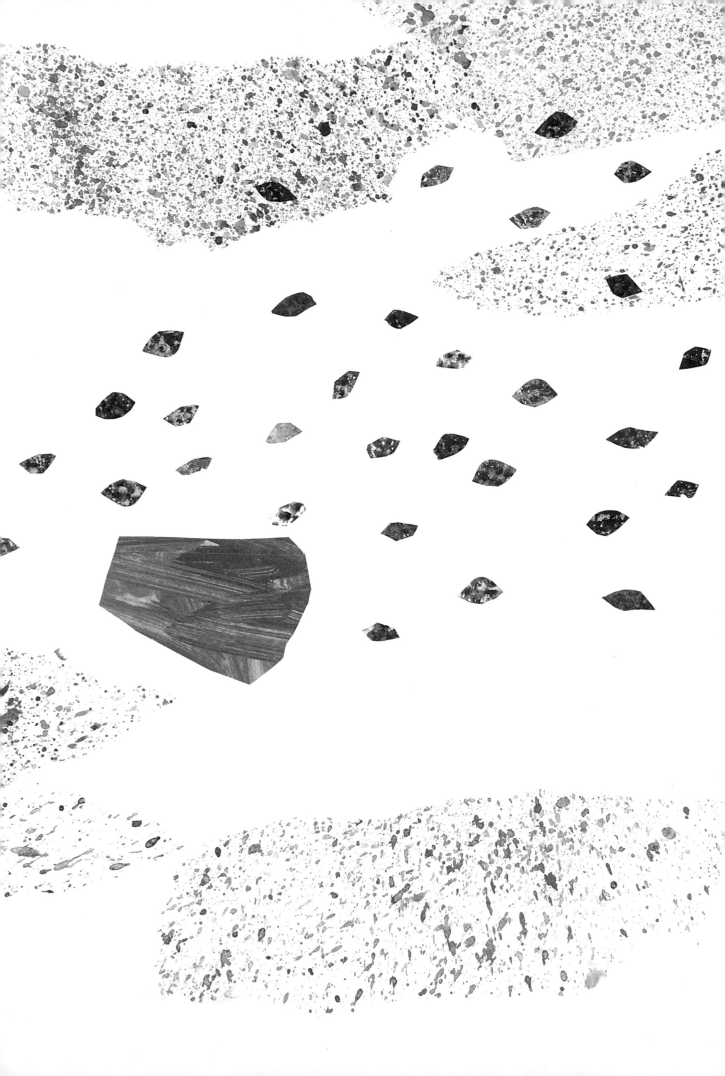